TALES FROM
Pinocchio

TALES FROM

Pinocchio

Helen Rossendale

illustrated by

Graham Philpot

PAVILION
CHILDREN'S

To Henrietta
G.P

This edition first published in the United Kingdom in 2010
by Pavilion Children's Books
an imprint of Anova Books Group Ltd
10 Southcombe Street
London W14 0RA

A CIP catalogue record for this book is available from the British Library.
ISBN 9781843651475
Repro by Mission Productions Ltd
Printed by Craft Print

CONTENTS

Chapter One
Pinocchio Comes to Life   6

Chapter Two
Pinocchio Breaks His Promise   16

Chapter Three
Pinocchio Meets the Fox and the Cat   26

Chapter Four
Pinocchio is Rescued by The Blue Fairy   38

Chapter Five
Pinocchio in Trouble   48

Chapter Six
Pinocchio Goes to School   57

Chapter Seven
Pinocchio Discovers the Perils of Playland   68

Chapter Eight
Pinocchio Becomes a Real Boy   78

Pinocchio Comes to Life

Once upon a time there was a piece of wood. It belonged to an old carpenter known as Mr Cherry because he had a small, shiny, red nose. One wintry afternoon, Mr Cherry decided to carve his piece of wood into a table leg. As he lifted his axe to slice off the rough bark, he heard a tiny voice. "Please don't strike me," it begged. Mr Cherry looked all around, but he was quite alone. "Must be my imagination," he muttered and

struck the wood with his axe. This time the voice cried out. "Stop! You're hurting me." The voice had come from the piece of wood! Mr Cherry was so shocked he collapsed on the floor and his cherry-red nose turned quite blue.

Just then there was a knock at the door. It was Mr Cherry's old friend, Geppetto. He too was a carpenter and he wore a yellow wig. Naughty children sometimes called him Mr Omelette-Head, which made Geppetto very angry.

"Whatever's the matter?" exclaimed Geppetto, finding his friend lying in a heap. Mr Cherry began mumbling a reply, but Geppetto was far too excited to listen. "I've had a fine idea," he announced. "I'm going to make a puppet that will dance and turn somersaults in the air."

"Bravo, Mr Omelette-Head!" cried the piece of

wood. Of course, Geppetto thought Mr Cherry had said this and so he lost his temper. The two old men started to fight, but their scuffle did not last long and soon they were shaking hands.

As a friendly gesture, Mr Cherry gave Geppetto the mysterious piece of wood so that he could make the puppet he had been talking about.

Geppetto rushed home. "I shall call my puppet Pinocchio," he said. But as he worked, strange things started to happen. As he carved the eyes, they began to blink. As he carved the nose, it began to grow and as he carved the mouth, it laughed at him and stuck out its tongue.

Geppetto could not believe his eyes, but carried on working nonetheless. He carved the body, the neck, the arms, the hands, the legs and the feet. Then, as Geppetto put the puppet together, it reached out and grabbed his wig. "Oh my!" gasped Geppetto. "You're such a naughty puppet."

Pinocchio jumped down onto the floor, danced around the room and ran out into the street.

Geppetto chased after Pinocchio but he was too slow. "Catch him, someone. Catch him!" cried Geppetto. Pinocchio clattered over the cobbles and ran straight into the arms of a policeman. Picking Pinocchio up by his nose, the policeman returned him to Geppetto.

"Just wait until I get you home!" scolded Geppetto, as he shook his naughty puppet. The people who had gathered to watch accused the old man of cruelty to puppets. So the policeman led Geppetto away to spend the night in prison, leaving Pinocchio free to skip home!

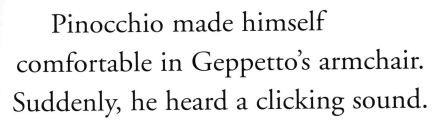

Pinocchio made himself comfortable in Geppetto's armchair. Suddenly, he heard a clicking sound.

He looked up and saw a cricket creeping up the wall.

"Who are you?" asked Pinocchio. "Why, I am the Talking Cricket," replied the little green insect. "And I have a warning for you. If you are rude and ungrateful to your father, and if you run away from home, then you shall come to no good."

"Oh be quiet you miserable, croaking Cricket," snapped Pinocchio. Then – grabbing a mallet – he hurled it at the wall. Now, Pinocchio had meant nothing more than to startle the Cricket, but the mallet struck him squarely and the poor creature, who had been simply trying to offer some good advice, was flattened. Pinocchio felt terrible about what had happened.

Pinocchio Breaks His Promise

Pinocchio felt lonely without Geppetto, and wretched for squashing the Cricket. But he was also hungry so he went out into the rain to beg for food. Each time he knocked on someone's door he was greeted with angry cries to go away. Pinocchio trudged back home. Exhausted, soaking wet and still very

17

hungry, he sat by the fire to dry himself. Before long he fell asleep.

In the morning, Pinocchio was woken by Geppetto's angry voice. "I'm home!" he cried. "But no thanks to you." Then Geppetto looked down at Pinocchio's feet and saw two burnt stumps. "Oh, whatever has happened?" he sobbed.

Pinocchio told Geppetto his sorry story: how he had not meant to kill the Cricket, how no one had given him food, and how his feet had burned to cinders as he slept.

Geppetto gave Pinocchio some pears to eat, then he carved two new feet and fixed them to Pinocchio's legs.

"Oh thank you, Daddy!" cried Pinocchio. "I promise I'll be a good puppet and I'll go to school. But I'll need some clothes to wear."

So Geppetto made Pinocchio a fine suit out of coloured paper, a pair of shoes out of bark and a hat out of stale bread.

"There's just one other thing I will need," said Pinocchio. "An exercise book."

Now Geppetto had no money, but he loved his little puppet so much that he went straight out, sold his only coat and bought Pinocchio a book.

It was snowing when Pinocchio set off for school. 'Today I shall learn to read,' he thought.

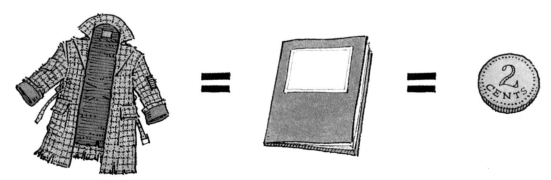

'Tomorrow I shall learn to write and the day after that I shall learn my numbers. Then I shall be able to earn lots of money and buy my daddy a new coat!'

But as he entered the village he was heard music and a man announcing: *'The Greatest Puppet Show on Earth!'* In an instant, he forgot his promise to Geppetto and sold his schoolbook for just two pence, the price of a ticket for the show.

Full of excitement, he stepped into the tent.

He gave not a single thought to his poor father, shivering at home without a coat.

The show had already started and the audience cheered the puppets as they sang and danced. But as soon as they caught sight of Pinocchio they called out, "Why, if it isn't Pinocchio! Come and join your wooden brothers!" Pinocchio leapt onto the stage and the other puppets crowded around him.

At that moment, the Showman appeared. He was a huge, ugly man with a long, black beard. "Who has dared to disturb my show?" he boomed, pointing an angry finger at Pinocchio.

"Tonight," he continued, "you will come to my tent to explain yourself. But now, ladies and gentlemen, on with the show!"

In the evening, Pinocchio was led to the tent where the Showman was preparing his supper.

"Throw that miserable Pinocchio on the fire!" he bellowed.

"But, Master," pleaded one of the puppets. "Why?"

"Because I said so!" snapped the angry Showman.

The puppets reluctantly pushed Pinocchio towards the flames: they were too scared to disobey. In despair, Pinocchio cried out, "Oh save me, Daddy!"

On hearing these words, the Showman suddenly remembered his own father with great fondness. He took pity on Pinocchio and decided to spare him. "Does your daddy love you?" he asked.

"Oh yes!" replied Pinocchio. "He sold his only coat to buy me a schoolbook. That's how much he loves me."

"Here, take these five gold coins home to him," said the Showman. "You are indeed lucky to have such a father."

Pinocchio Meets the Fox and the Cat

Pinocchio had much to be grateful for. He thanked the Showman a thousand times, said a fond farewell to all the puppets, and set out for home with his five gold coins. How pleased Geppetto would be!

He had not gone far when he met a lame fox and a blind cat, begging by the roadside. "Good morning, little puppet," whined the Fox. "Can you spare us a penny or two?"

Foolishly, Pinocchio told the strangers that he had five gold coins for his father and that he was returning home to go to school.

"School!" hissed the Cat. "You don't want to go to school. It is studying that made us lame and blind!"

"Why don't you come with us?' asked the Fox. 'We know a place where you could turn those five gold coins into five thousand! It is called the Field of Miracles and if you bury your coins there, they will grow into money trees overnight!"

Pinocchio's eyes became as wide as saucers. 'With that sort of money I could buy Daddy one hundred new coats and a schoolbook for every day of the year!' he thought. He turned to the Fox and the Cat and said, "Yes! I shall come with you."

After walking all day, the three decided to stop off at the Red Crab Inn. The Fox and the Cat feasted on fish, chicken, rabbit, partridge eggs, and cheese but Pinocchio, whose mind was on other things, only nibbled at some bread.

"Now let us go to our rooms and rest," said the Fox. "We'll continue our journey at midnight."

As the clock struck twelve, Pinocchio leapt out of bed. "But where are the Fox and the Cat?" he asked. The innkeeper told Pinocchio his companions had already gone and then asked for one gold coin as payment for the bill.

Pinocchio stumbled out into the darkness. He was drawn to a strange, green glow in the trees. "I am the ghost of the Talking Cricket," it said. "Do not trust the Fox and the Cat." But Pinocchio refused to listen and the ghost faded away, murmuring, "Beware of robbers, Pinocchio. Beware!"

"Robbers indeed!" scoffed Pinocchio, but just as

he said these words, two black figures, wrapped in coal sacks, came bounding towards him.

Quick as a flash, Pinocchio hid the four coins in his shoe and, as he stood up, the attackers grabbed him from behind. "Your money or your life!" they cried. "But I have no money!" protested Pinocchio.

The robbers did not believe him and this time they shouted,

"Your money or your father's life!" Their threat made Pinocchio very angry indeed. He stamped on the big one's bushy tail and bit the little one's furry paw and ran for his life into the woods. He had no time to realise who these robbers really were!

At the edge of the woods, by a little white cottage, the robbers caught up with Pinocchio. They bound him with ropes and tied him to the branch of a big oak tree. "We shall come back

tomorrow," they sneered. "By then you will tell us where your gold coins are."

But it was not the robbers who came for Pinocchio in the morning. Instead, he was loosened from his ropes and lifted down from the tree by a great falcon. He was placed gently in a coach made of golden pastry where he sank into the deep strawberry cushions. Then the coachman, a poodle dressed in a raspberry-red tailcoat and chocolate-brown breeches, ordered his fleet of sugar-white mice to take Pinocchio to the safety of the little white cottage.

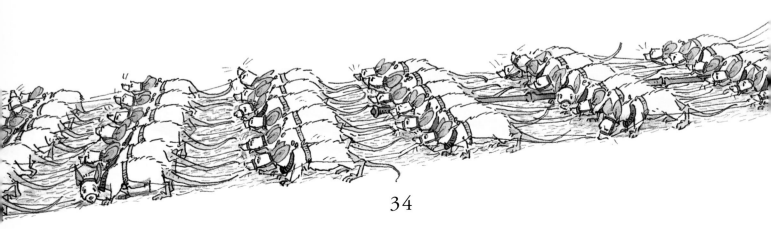

Pinocchio is Rescued by The Blue Fairy

The little white cottage belonged to the Blue Fairy and it was she who had seen poor Pinocchio hanging from the tree and had commanded her trusted servants to rescue him. She called for the best doctors in the neighbourhood – a crow, an owl and a talking cricket. They could not agree whether Pinocchio was dead or alive but the Cricket turned to the Blue Fairy and spoke gravely:

"Here is a most disobedient, wayward son who will surely make his father die of a broken heart," he said.

Suddenly, Pinocchio broke into sorrowful sobs.

"He's alive!" sighed the Blue Fairy and she sent the doctors away.

Pinocchio told the Blue Fairy everything. How the Showman had given him five gold coins, how the Fox and the Cat had tricked him and how he had been chased and tied up by robbers.

"Where are your gold coins now?" asked the Blue Fairy, kindly.

"I've lost them," answered Pinocchio. But this was a lie, for he had them in his shoe and, as soon as he spoke these words, his nose grew two inches longer!

"Where did you lose them?" asked the Fairy.

"In the woods," said Pinocchio. A second lie. His nose grew again!

"Then we shall search for them and they shall be found," said the Blue Fairy.

"Oh no," he replied. "I remember now, the robbers stole them." At this third lie, his nose grew so long that it touched the window pane!

The Fairy looked at him and laughed.

"Why are you laughing at me?" asked Pinocchio.

"I am laughing at the lies you have told, Pinocchio. For each time you lie, your nose grows a little longer!"

Full of shame, Pinocchio tried to run from the room but his long nose stopped him from getting through the door! The Fairy left him alone for a while to teach him a lesson, but then she clapped her hands and a flock of woodpeckers pecked away at Pinocchio's nose until it was back to its normal size.

"How good you are to me." said Pinocchio. "I love you."

"I love you, too," answered the Blue Fairy. "I shall be your darling sister." Then she promised to bring Pinocchio's father to the cottage that very evening. Full of joy, Pinocchio ran outside to wait for Geppetto.

But whom should he meet instead? The wicked Fox and Cat! For a second time, Pinocchio was fooled by their deceitful words and agreed to go with them to the Field of Miracles.

When they reached the lonely spot, Pinocchio dug holes for his four gold coins and covered them with earth.

"Now you must go away for twenty minutes," explained the Fox. "When you come back you'll see the first green shoots already covered in gold coins."

But when Pinocchio returned there were no green shoots. There was only a scraggy parrot who told Pinocchio that the Fox and the Cat had dug up the coins and run away.

Pinocchio could not believe it. He dug a hole as big as a haystack but the parrot was right. The coins were gone!

In desperation, Pinocchio ran to a nearby town to tell the judge about the evil robbers. The judge, a portly gorilla, listened patiently to Pinocchio's story. Then, clearing his throat, he announced, "This poor fellow has been robbed. Take him to prison, immediately!"

Pinocchio spent four long months in jail in this strange, cruel town. He counted down the days until he was set free and could find his way back to the kind Blue Fairy who had promised to reunite him with his dear father.

Pinocchio in Trouble

On the day he was let out of jail, Pinocchio ran as fast as he could back to the Blue Fairy's house. The journey was long and the day was hot. So he leapt over a fence to pick some juicy grapes but he landed in a trap.

Pinocchio screamed for help. And the farmer, who had set the trap, came running over to see his catch.

"So it's you who has been stealing my chickens!" he grunted.

"No sir!" pleaded Pinocchio. "I

49

only wanted a few grapes."

The farmer opened the trap, seized Pinocchio and chained him to a kennel. "You shall be my new guard dog," he bellowed.

Later that night, Pinocchio saw four prowling polecats in the darkness. When the polecats had skulked into the chicken coop, Pinocchio quickly bolted the door and barked as loud as he could.

The farmer rushed out in his nightshirt. He was so pleased that Pinocchio had caught the chicken thieves that he hugged him warmly and let him go.

Pinocchio ran through the night to the Fairy's house. But when he reached the edge of the wood, there was no sign of the little white cottage. There was only a simple white grave with an inscription that read: 'Here lies the blue-haired child who died of sorrow on being deserted by her little brother, Pinocchio.'

Although Pinocchio could not read the words,

he knew at once the horrible meaning of the little grave. He had lost his beloved Blue Fairy.

"Please, dear Fairy," he sobbed. "Come back to me and tell me where I may find my daddy."

Just then, a pigeon flew over Pinocchio's head. It was as large as a turkey. "I have come to take you to your father," cooed the pigeon.

Holding tightly to the pigeon's feathers, Pinocchio was whisked into the air.

"Your father is at sea," said the pigeon. "He has made a little boat so that he might search the whole world for you." The pigeon flew all day until, at dusk, they reached the coast. It was a stormy night and Pinocchio saw a tiny boat being tossed by the waves. He dived into the water and

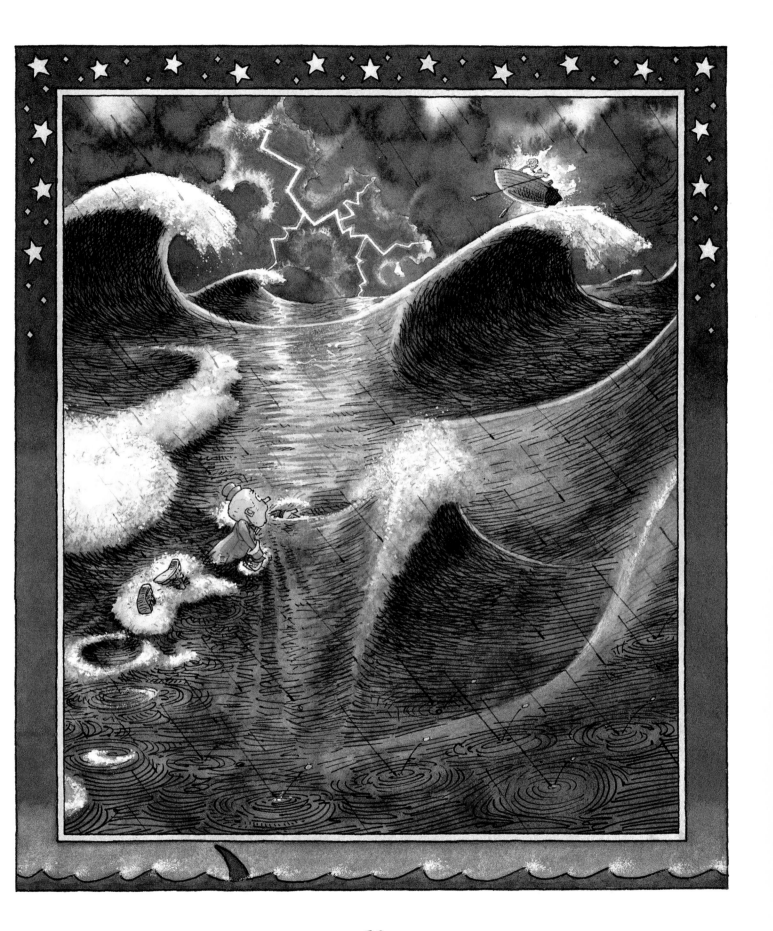

swam as fast as he could towards the boat.
Pinocchio swam all night but he could not reach
his father.

By daybreak, he could swim no more, and was
washed up on an island. Suddenly, a friendly
dolphin popped its head above the waves.

"Have you seen my daddy?" pleaded Pinocchio.

"No," said the dolphin. "But there is a great
shark that lurks in these
waters. I fear it has
swallowed up your
father."

Pinocchio headed
inland. A little woman
was coming towards him
carrying two buckets of
water. Pinocchio asked
her politely for a drink.

"Gladly," said the little
woman. Then she invited

Pinocchio to her house for something to eat. "For you must be hungry, too," she said. The woman set down a bowl of hearty soup. When he had finished eating, Pinocchio looked up to thank the kind woman. He saw her smile and knew her at once.

"Blue Fairy!" he cried. "You have come back to me!"

"Yes," she replied. "Because I could see how truly sorry you were to have lost me." The Fairy was just as lovely as ever, but she was no longer a little girl.

"You have grown into a beautiful woman," said Pinocchio. "From now on I shall call you Mummy." Then he whispered, "Will I ever grow up into a real boy?"

"Yes," said the Fairy. "If you are good, always tell the truth and study hard, then I promise that one day you will find your father and become a real boy."

Pinocchio Goes to School

When Pinocchio started school, he was determined not to let the Blue Fairy down and he worked very hard. But alas, not all of his classmates were as studious and some of them were bullies.

One morning on his way to school, Pinocchio was stopped by a gang. "A shark as big as a

mountain has been spotted in the sea," they said. "We're going to look. Want to come?"

Pinocchio wondered if this could be the shark that had swallowed up his father, and part of him wanted to go to the beach.

But he knew that he mustn't be late for school.

"It won't take long," they sneered, seeing Pinocchio's uncertainty. So he ran with the children to the beach but there was no sign of the shark.

"Where's the shark?" asked Pinocchio.

"Perhaps he's having breakfast," sniggered one of the bullies. "Geppetto and chips!"

Then they all roared with laughter and Pinocchio knew he had been tricked. He lost his temper and an angry fight broke out.

In the turmoil, a heavy book struck one of the boys and he fell onto the sand. The others ran off, leaving Pinocchio with his wounded classmate.

Just then two policemen came striding along

the beach with a big dog at their side. "What have we here?" said one of the officers. "Little puppet, are you responsible for this boy's injuries?"

"N-n-no sir," stammered Pinocchio.

"You had better come to the police station to explain yourself," grunted the other officer. And with that, they left the injured boy with some fishermen and marched Pinocchio back towards town.

"How ashamed I would be if the Blue Fairy saw me now," thought Pinocchio. He struggled free, ran back across the beach, and into the sea. The police dog bounded after him, but it could not swim.

It splashed furiously towards Pinocchio but, in

the deeper water, it began to sink. "Help!" barked the dog.

Pinocchio had his chance to escape, but he could not let the poor dog drown, so he pulled it back to the shore.

"You saved my life," panted the dog. "I shall never forget your kindness."

Pinocchio waded back into the water and swam towards the next bay. But suddenly he was caught in a huge net and hauled onto the sand. A strange-looking fisherman dragged the net into his cave where a cauldron of hot oil was bubbling. He tossed the fish in flour and fried them until they were crispy and golden. Pinocchio cowered in terror at the bottom of the net, awaiting his turn.

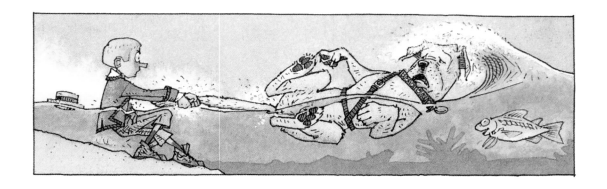

"Aha," boomed the fisherman. "I've never had puppet-fish before!"

Pinocchio screamed and struggled but it was useless and in an instant he had been smothered in flour. The fisherman was just about to drop him into the cauldron when the police dog came charging into the cave and seized Pinocchio from the fisherman's grasp.

"It was the smell of delicious fried fish that brought me here," woofed the dog. "But then I heard your screams and knew you were in danger. Climb onto my back and I'll take you home."

The Blue Fairy sat Pinocchio down at the kitchen table and looked at him solemnly. 'I am very saddened that you did not go to school today,' she said. "You must never let me down like this again."

"I won't," said Pinocchio. "I promise!" And, for a whole year, Pinocchio kept his promise. He went to school every day and he was always top of the class. He was given a big silver cup for being the best pupil of the year. The Blue Fairy was very, very proud of him.

BEST
PUPIL

Pinocchio Discovers the Perils of Playland

The Blue Fairy knew the best way to reward Pinocchio for his hard work and so planned a surprise for him.

"Tomorrow will be the day that you become a real boy", she said. "And to celebrate, we'll have a party!"

She gave Pinocchio invitations for the special breakfast party and he skipped out to deliver them. As he turned a corner, he saw his good friend Luciano sitting on the kerb.

"Hello," said Pinocchio. "What are you doing?"

"I'm waiting for the coach to take me to Playland," he replied. "Do you want to come with me?"

"No thank you," said Pinocchio, politely. "I have these invitations to deliver for my breakfast party. Tomorrow I'm going to become a real boy."

Tomorrow Pinocchio will become a real boy. You are invited to a very special Breakfast Party to celebrate this wonderful day

"But Playland is much more fun than silly old breakfast parties!" said Luciano. "Look! Here comes the coach now!"

And sure enough, a coach came rumbling into view. The coach was pulled by the strangest-looking donkeys Pinocchio had ever seen! Some were grey and brown but others were multi-coloured and they all wore white leather boots. The coach was crammed with children and alongside it strode the coachman, who was broader

than he was tall, with a face as red as a tomato.

Luciano clambered onto the crowded coach. Pinocchio hesitated, but he couldn't stop thinking about all the wonderful toys and games there might be in Playland.

In a flash, he dropped his invitations, and jumped onto the nearest donkey. As it moved off, Pinocchio thought he heard it say, "Don't go, Pinocchio."

When they reached Playland, Pinocchio leapt off his donkey. By now it was crying and it spoke again, this time more urgently. "Please don't go in, Pinocchio. You'll end up like me!" But Pinocchio had already joined the mad rush through the gates.

Pinocchio spent five fabulous months in Playland. There were games and funfairs and parties. All kinds of entertainers came to amuse the children and the place was overflowing with happiness.

But then, one morning, Pinocchio had a nasty

surprise. When he looked in the mirror he discovered that he had grown donkey ears! He pulled a bag over his ears and went to Luciano's room.

When Luciano opened his door, Pinocchio gasped to see that he too had a bag on his head. When they realised they both had donkey ears they laughed and laughed. But then they began to walk on all fours and make loud braying noises. In no time at all, they had both become donkeys!

Just at that moment, the coachman arrived and, throwing a rough loop of rope around each of their necks, he took them to market. That was the last Pinocchio ever saw of Luciano.

Pinocchio was sold to a circus. He was kept in a dingy stable and fed on straw. Every day, he spent hours learning how to jump through hoops and dance the polka.

Then came his first performance. The crowd

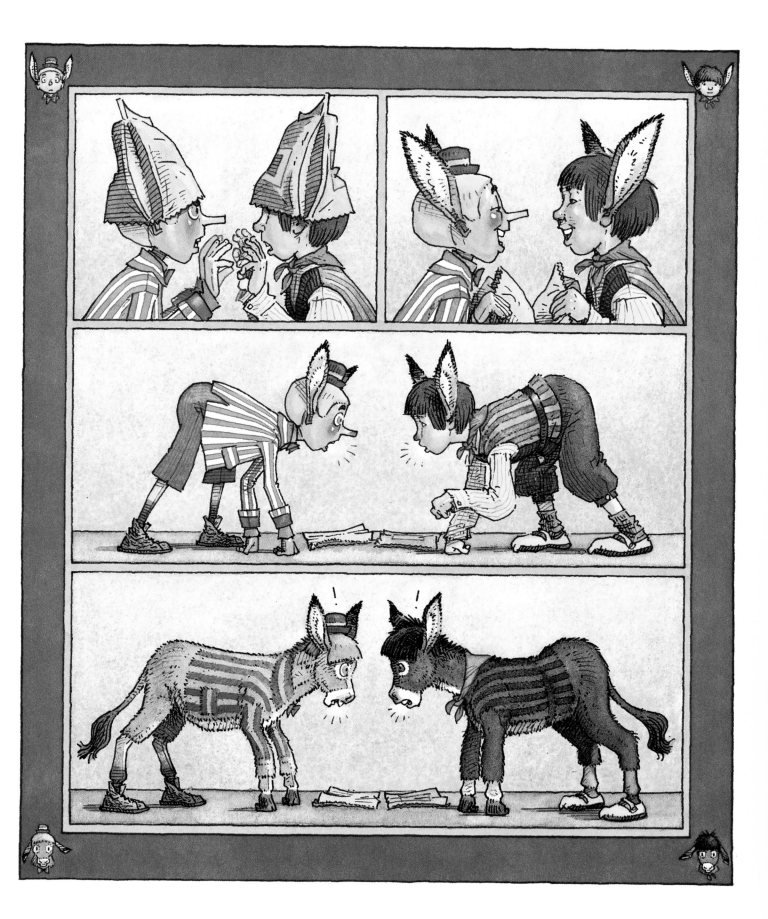

loved his routine and the ringmaster lifted the hoop higher and higher. But disaster struck when the hoop was raised too high and Pinocchio fell to the ground with a thud.

"Lame donkeys are no good to me!" bellowed the ringmaster, so he took Pinocchio back to the market. "Old nag going cheap!" he hollered.

"I'll give you five pennies," grunted a rough-looking fellow. "I'll use his skin to repair the big drum in the village band." Pinocchio's new owner led him to the shore, tied a stone around his neck and pushed him into the water. "I'll pull you back up when you're drowned," he cackled. "Then I'll skin you for my drum!"

Pinocchio was saved from drowning. A shoal of fish nibbled away his donkey skin and Pinocchio swam free.

Pinocchio Becomes a Real Boy

Soon, Pinocchio caught sight of a goat standing on a rock. It had a beautiful blue, curly coat – just like the Blue Fairy's hair – and it was pointing towards a huge shark swimming towards them. Pinocchio knew this must be the shark that had swallowed his daddy.

"Swim for your life!" bleated the goat. But the monstrous fish swallowed poor Pinocchio in one massive gulp.

Inside the shark, Pinocchio found himself in a long, dark tunnel. There was a flickering light. Pinocchio walked steadily towards it and, as he

drew closer, he saw a figure sitting by candlelight at a small table. The old man turned slowly towards Pinocchio. It was Geppetto!

"Daddy, I've found you at last!" cried Pinocchio. Geppetto could hardly speak; he was so overcome with joy. Father and son stayed in each other's arms for a very long time and, through his tears of happiness, Pinocchio told Geppetto about every one of his sorry adventures from that fateful day when he sold his schoolbook outside the puppet theatre.

Then Geppetto told Pinocchio his story. "I've been trapped here for two years," he explained. "Just after I was swallowed up, the shark gulped down a large ship and I've been living off its stores of food. But now there is very little left."

"We must find a way out!" said Pinocchio, firmly. He took Geppetto's hand and they clambered back along the shark's long, bony throat. "We'll be able to get out the way we came

81

in," Pinocchio reassured his father. When they reached its mouth, they found that the shark was sleeping with its jaws wide open and they could see the moonlit sky beyond the rows of fearsome teeth.

They scrambled over the teeth and with Geppetto clinging to his back, Pinocchio swam out into the inky-black sea.

Pinocchio became very tired and he could barely swim another stroke. In the nick of time, a tuna fish who had followed them out of the shark's stomach came along and carried them to the shore.

Pinocchio and Geppetto set off along a narrow path. They walked for hours until finally they

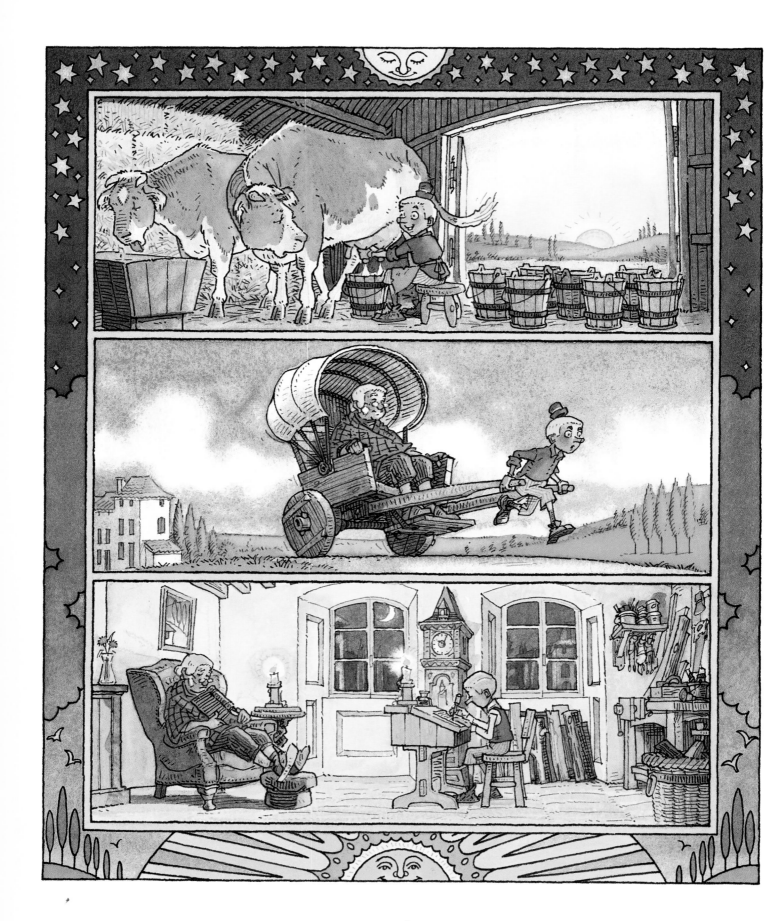

came to a familiar cobbled street and found themselves outside Geppetto's house!

Every day, from dawn till dusk, Pinocchio looked after his father, who was still very frail. He took a job working for a local farmer. When he had earned enough, he bought a new coat for his father and an exercise book for himself. He didn't have time to go to school, but he practised reading

and writing every evening after supper.

Little by little, Geppetto's health improved. It made Pinocchio so glad to see his father's strength return. Before long, Geppetto was well enough to start woodcarving once again.

Then, one night, Pinocchio saw the Blue Fairy in a dream. "You have been a brave puppet, Pinocchio," she said, softly. "You rescued your father and nursed him back to health. In return for your good heart, I promise that tomorrow you will find true happiness."

The next morning, Pinocchio leapt out of bed and as usual he went to the bathroom mirror but, instead of the face of a puppet, he saw the smiling face of a little boy! Squealing with delight, he ran downstairs to find Geppetto.

Geppetto kissed his son. "It is your kindness that has turned you into a little boy," he laughed. "And I am proud to have you as my son, darling Pinocchio."

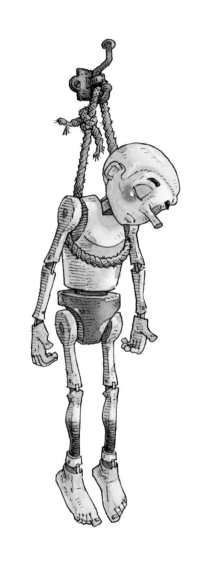

And, as for the puppet, it was nothing
more than a piece of wood.